THE VAMPIRE VANASHEZ

The Transition

I'm a vampire. But I wasn't always like this. I would like to say that my life was fine before I became this thing, but it wasn't. I lost all of my money in the stock market crash of 1929. I was a homeless vagabond after that. Even so, I thought that somehow things would turn around. They did, but not the way I hoped. I was simply looking for a place to sleep one night. That's when he appeared. I saw a big man wearing a coat and hat. With a gleam in his eye. I could almost feel evil resonating from him. I knew he was trouble, so I turned and started walking away. This man somehow leapt over my head and landed silently in front of me! That shocked me. So did the fangs, when I finally saw them. By then he was too close for me to escape.

"I've been watching you, Victor Vanashez", he spoke. "You've lost everything. But I can give you power. Lasting power, the kind you will never lose."

"Are you a vampire?", I asked.

"Yes. It matters little whether you believe this now or not. You shall, soon enough. My name is Steven Burns. I am your new master!"

This creature named Steven had my arm in his grip. He was too strong to fight, but I was trying anyway. I hadn't lost the will to live after all. Not that it mattered. Steven let out a hiss and bit my neck. I still remember the sting of pain. It felt as if my warmth was being drained. To my surprise, I remained conscious. He was sucking blood out through my new wound. I think I felt my heartbeat slow, but it never stopped. He finally released me, and I fell to the ground. What little light there was that night began to dim in my eyes. I figured I was dying. Suddenly I felt a strange surge of strength within me. I groaned and rose to my feet. Steven seemed pleased with this, as he was smiling. I was standing, but felt some pain within me. I didn't know at the time that it was my body adjusting to the changes being made. When a vampire takes a certain amount of blood from a person, it 'turns' the individual. Changes them on a genetic level into something that looks human, but isn't. I only screamed once, then it was over. I could feel the fangs in my mouth. And despite the darkness, I could see very clearly. In fact, all of my senses were more acute. And I knew then that my life as Victor Vanashez had come to an end.

"Excellent", said Steven. "You survived the process. You are now mine to command. A creature of the night; another one added to my ever-growing army. Some vampires only want to kill. But not I, I wish to conquer. And soon, my army of the night will come out of the shadows and rule over mankind!"
"I understand. It feels like I understand everything!"
"Of course", continued Steven. "When you turned, a part of me became a part of your mind. You now know what I know."
"But...this is wrong!" I was somehow able to resist his demonic influence.
"What's this? Mutiny, so soon? It is unheard of. You had nothing to live for. I could understand if you did, some people like that are quite resistant. So how can this be? Unless..." Steven looked up as though he was studying the night sky. I took this opportunity to run away from him. To my surprise, I moved far more swiftly than I ever

had before. Steven noticed this as well.

"I command you to return to me! No? So be it. I know now why you can resist me. But I will find you, Victor. You can not hide from me for long. You will be mine!"

I got as far away from Steven as I could. I hid under a bridge while I tried to make sense of the new information in my brain. When I was bitten, Steven's knowledge of vampires was transferred to me. My senses were now enhanced as a result of my transformation. I was under a barrage of new scents. This made me realize that Steven could most likely track me by my scent. So I left the bridge and found myself wandering through a graveyard. I now knew that I should avoid the sun's rays, as they would be like a slow poison to my new system. I broke into a mausoleum and stayed there while more information was revealed to me. I knew that I had to have human blood at least once a month to stay strong. I could shapeshift, but only to a limited degree. I certainly could not become mist or a bat, as those seemed impossible. But I could grow wings or resemble a type of wolf. Before the sun rose, I realized why I could resist Steven. Another piece of knowledge passed from him to me. A vampire's powers are at their weakest on the fourth night after the full moon. And that's when he bit me! He knew this, but had foolishly not kept track of the lunar cycle as he was busy building his army. So he didn't have the power to command me. I would have been too weak to resist, but I was new and at the peak of my own power. Before I went to sleep I realized that while this was a curse, there were some good things about it. My old life was far from good, perhaps this new existence would be better. Only time would tell.

-THE END.

The War Begins

It was the year 1930. I, Victor Vanashez, had successfully hidden myself for one year from the creature that made me what I am. A vampire. It was easier than I thought it would be. Mostly because when Steven Burns had bitten me, much of what he knew became embedded in my mind. This helped me to think like him and to stay a step ahead of him. I even moved to a different state to avoid him. I believe he wanted me to join the vampire army he was building. And even though I had changed from human to vampire, I still felt essentially the same about many things. I had to feed on human blood once a month, but I only went after those I considered to be a blight on society. And I removed them, instead of changing them into vampires. I had no interest in joining Steven or his 'cause'. Still, I figured my luck would only hold out for so long. I made it through that year without incident, but 1931 was a different story.

I was out one night looking for a corrupt human to feed on. I observed those around me at night and knew who the worst among them were. I usually had a couple of targets picked out for elimination. I was hunting a man named George that night. Suddenly, I caught a scent. It was the scent of a vampire. No, it was two of them! I abandoned George to see what the pair of creatures were up to. I could smell them, but didn't see them. Even with my now enhanced vision. Were they hiding? If so, had they been hunting too? Perhaps, but three of us in the same small area? I didn't buy it. They were hunting, all right. But their prey was most likely me.
"Alright, fellows", I said. "I know you're there. You smell like landfill." One of them hissed in response, which gave away his position. He must have known that, because next thing I knew, he was on me. He jumped down from the tree he was perched in and landed on my back.

I ran backwards to slam my attacker into a tree. It hurt him but didn't dislodge him from me. So I changed my fingernail into a claw via my shapeshifting power and poked his eye. He howled in pain and released me. I broke a branch off of the tree. It was big enough to use as a weapon. Since my adversary was still blinded, I had the chance to aim for his heart. Sticking wood through a vampires' heart effectively terminates their connection to this world. It releases their soul from the body. So that's what I did, walked softly and carried a big stick. Right through his heart. That killed the first one. The second vampire was still hiding.
"Why attack me?", I asked. "Who are you working for?" I

already knew what the answer must be.

"I am called Shawl", answered the remaining vampire, from behind the trees. "I belong to Steven Burns. He still wishes to recruit you into his army. There are no hard feelings, if you return with me now."

"Tell him thanks, but no thanks. I work alone. In fact, maybe I should be working on taking his army apart."

"Have it your way, Victor. You'll be sorry." With that, he was gone. After that encounter, I moved again. But it did give me the idea to start doing away with any and all vampires. After all, I was committed to disposing of evil. So now I would start at the source.

-THE END.

Playing the Game

My name is Victor Vanashez and I'm still a vampire. I

have a feeling I always will be. I'm not happy about it, but that's how it is. I have no love for other vampires. In fact, I've been successfully killing them for three years now. The year is 1934 and I have a feeling that the general populace of vampires knows by now that I don't play well with others. They've stopped trying to recruit me for their vampire army. Now they just want me dead. The feeling is mutual. One vampire in particular has evaded me pretty well. Other than my 'master', Steven Burns. The one I'm referring to goes by the name of Roderick Shawl. Either we keep missing each other or he's avoiding me. Which makes sense to me since I want to kill him. But now I had an idea of where he was. I saw a good friend of his in town and I thought maybe they were here together. I keep a journal about my enemies and Shawl was near the top of my list. I was hoping he'd be my next target.

I kept a lookout for any of his friends in the local park at night. They sometimes went there looking for food. Humans or animals, they didn't really care. On that night I got lucky. Shawl's friend Tommy showed up. He was too busy hunting a stray cat to notice me at first. When I ran towards him he heard me. He also fell to the ground quickly so that my momentum carried me over him. Tommy was a good fighter. I saw him check my hands to make sure I wasn't carrying a stake to kill him with. When he found none, he hissed and leapt at me. This time I used his momentum and spun him to the ground. I held him down by his neck with my left hand. I raised my right arm in the air swiftly enough for the hidden stake to fly up out of my sleeve. With my right hand I caught it. I brought it down too fast for Tommy to stop me from pounding it into his heart. The creature howled in disbelief that the fight was over...and so was his life. Tommy was good, but I was better.

The next night I went back to the park thinking that Shawl or some other vampire would show up to see what had happened to Tommy. I saw a happy couple strolling the park late at night and followed them. I figured if there were other vampires around, they could not resist this set up. Surprisingly, the couple got out of the park unscathed. It began to dawn on me that even though Roderick and Tommy were friends, Shawl must have considered his friends expendable. If Shawl suspected that it was I who killed Tommy, he'd probably just leave this town to avoid confrontation. He had lived a long time and planned on living a lot longer. Shawl was smart all right. I stayed another night just to make sure, but there was no sign of any of my kind around. I must have guessed it right. Steven Burns picked his top men pretty well. I was good at this game, but apparently Shawl was just a little bit better. I was going to need more practice before I actually went up against this one. Because if this is a game, then it's a game I'm planning on winning.

The End.

Death in a Graveyard

In 1936, I finally found an ally in my war against vampires. Despite the fact that we were both vampires ourselves. I'm Victor Vanashez and my partner was Taylor Stitch. Taylor had been turned by Steven Burns five years earlier than I was. He had even begun to follow his ideology; his idea that vampires should rule and all humans should be exterminated or become slaves. Then something unexpected happened. Taylor began to care for a human named Kelly. She was the one who reawakened Taylor's human feelings. Steven was not going to put up with this. So he killed Kelly. Which drove Taylor to rebellion. I met Taylor while on the trail of Steven. Instead of fighting, we got to talking. That's when he revealed all of this to me. We decided that we would work together to destroy Steven Burns and his plans for mankind. But there was one loose end to take care of before we could get to Steven. A vampire named Shawl was one of Steven's most loyal officers. Taylor and I both hated him.

Shawl was a slippery character. I had been trying to get my hands on him for years. He had a habit of staying one step ahead of me. But now I had a partner in my war, and things would be different. We got a lucky break in 1937. I heard through the vampire grapevine that some of Shawl's foot soldiers were in a small town. They had already killed a few people there during their night time hunts. What I didn't know was that Roderick Shawl was there with them.

Taylor and I were vampire hunting one night in that small town. We ended up finding three of them in a cemetery. I recognized all three of them. Lucky, Shiny and Shawl. They had gone after three humans who decided to take a shortcut through the graveyard on the wrong night. They had just caught up to the humans when Taylor and I caught up to them. It must have been quite a sight for the people involved, five vampires at once. They took off and I'm sure they never returned to that place again.

Lucky still had the scar on his chest that I had given him. Vampires don't usually scar as we heal quickly. But this one was made with a wooden stake. What can I say, I missed. And he was still alive. Shiny got his name because when he was turned into a vampire, his skin turned white. And stayed that way. His hair, too. So he was shiny, in the moonlight. Not that any of this mattered to my partner Taylor; he just wanted to see them dead. So did I. So we went to work.

Shawl spotted us first and shouted an order to the other two. These two didn't carry wooden stakes, as they were after humans and not vampires. But Taylor and I did. Taylor had turned his feet into talons and was working on shredding as much of Shiny's hide as he could. I found myself in a wrestling match with Lucky, who recognized me.

"Victor", he said. "This time I'll finish you."

"Good luck, Lucky", was my reply.

Shawl was on the sidelines watching events unfold. I thought for sure that he'd take off. He always was a survivor. But for some reason he was still there. Maybe he thought he'd watch me die. I found that scenario unlikely. Taylor had easily gotten the best of Shiny. He was now standing over the bloodied vampire, holding his wooden stake. He brought it down with a great speed. He found his target, Shiny's heart, and Shiny was no more. I was still wrestling with Lucky when I saw this. I also heard Taylor's 'victory-howl'. I had warned him not to do that, as it distracted him and also could be heard by humans. But Taylor always did what he wanted. And from my vantage point I finally realized why Shawl hadn't left. He had brought a stake of his own! I should have known this was too easy. I tried to warn him, but Lucky reshaped his hand to a size that would fit in my mouth. I was muted, and Shawl was bearing down on my partner.

Shawl attacked Taylor from behind. The wooden stake went right through his back. But it must have missed his heart, as he was still alive. This didn't bother Shawl. He struck two more times with his weapon. His third strike did find Taylor's heart. He tried to cling to what life he had left, but it was not to be. I watched my partner fall for the final time. That angered me enough to give me strength. I threw Lucky off of me...fifteen feet into the air. I grabbed for my stake, hidden under my pant leg near my foot. I got it out and into position just in time for Lucky to come down and land on it...heart-first. I still had good alm, despite my anger. Lucky's luck had just run out. I wish I could say the same for Shawl. When I looked up from my kill, he was nowhere to be seen. I knew that sucker was fast, but this...I could have sworn he saw Lucky die. But he was already gone. Not even my enhanced senses could track him. But no matter. For what he had done, I hated him even more. I buried

11

Taylor there in that cemetery. Then I vowed that Shawl would get his. He would pay for his crimes, even if I had to track him all the way to Hell.

THE END.

Soldiers

By late 1939 I had heard of a war that was going on in Europe. It figures; people can never get along together for too long. Not that vampires are much better. I'm a vampire by the name of Victor. I had taken it upon myself to eradicate whatever vampires I could, unless I found them to be like myself. Only feeding when necessary, not trying to destroy or corrupt humanity further than it already was. I just wanted to continue my existence, as it was all I really had.

By late 1941 the war had reached America. As I thought it would eventually. These fools were going to destroy each other; they didn't need vampires to do it for them. I was still hunting the vampire named Roderick Shawl. I'd had a few skirmishes with him, but nothing major. Except for the fact that he'd killed an old partner of mine. I was a vampire, but Shawl was evil. He lived to do the bidding of his master, Steven Burns. Burns had tried being my master too, but that didn't work for me.

In 1942 I caught up to another of Shawl's lieutenants. He called himself Vrax. I only caught his name once before ripping out his throat and putting a wooden stake through his heart. I did it in that order so Shawl would know that he suffered some first. I thought perhaps I could anger Shawl into making a mistake that would allow me to finally take him down. No such luck. I'm sure he heard what happened to Vrax, but he left that city before I could catch him. Like so many times before. In the next year, I interrupted a late night battle in this new war. I killed a few of America's enemies that night. But my bloodied appearance startled a young American soldier, and he shot me. First time that had happened to me. The bullet tore a hole in my leg. Fortunately, I was able to shift the shape of my leg and heal it pretty quickly. Still, the wound angered me and I attacked the man. Another first happened that night. I knew how to turn men into vampires, but had never done so. Until now.

I'm not certain why I did it. Maybe I missed my partner, Taylor. But when I turned this man named Randall, he was given parts of my memories. To my surprise, he decided that he would aid me in destroying the evil vampires. After he figured out what was happening to him, that is. Perhaps I could only 'create' good vampires. This idea intrigued me. Randall and I went missing from America's war that night. We had our own war to win. In the Spring of 1944, we were finally closing in on Shawl and his men. But it turned out to be an ambush! We

13

were separated and each had two evil vampires to fight. Or so I thought. I ended up killing mine, but it took awhile. And I lost my left ear, but that would grow back. When I made my way into the building that Randall had entered, I heard Shawl's voice, near a far exit.

"You're too late, Victor". I looked and saw the slain bodies of the two evil vampires. Randall had killed them. But Shawl was there, a piece of information we did not have. I saw the body of my newest partner on the floor. Missing an eye, and a wooden stake through his heart.

The distraction caused by seeing Randall dead allowed Shawl to escape once again. But I kept my wits this time. I knew Randall had been killed very recently. That meant there was still time to try something desperate. I pulled the stake out of him. You only have five minutes after a vampire is staked to try to bring him back. After that, the soul can't come back to the body. But within five minutes, the rift could be repaired. A fact I learned from Steven Burns when he bit me. It was good to have some of his knowledge in my brain. I had nearly forgotten this information. Luck was on my side for once. I stared at Randall's corpse for a full minute, but then he breathed again! He was in pain and shocked to learn that he was still alive. I took him back to the graveyard we had been staying at. It only took three nights for him to fully recover from his ordeal. Randall was a tough one. I was glad to have him at my side. Plus, Shawl thought he was dead, which could be an advantage for us.

"Next time, Victor", said Randall. "Next time we bury that demon, Shawl." I believed him. It felt like all wars would be coming to an end soon. Which finally gave me something to smile about.

-The End-

The War Ends?

It was the year 1945 and my war on vampires was still on. Well, mine and Randall's. My name is Victor Vanashez. Randall Partz was my partner. I made him a vampire and he decided to join me in my war. He was originally a soldier in the great war that was still ongoing. He had also semi-retired from our war after he was killed. Luckily, I was able to bring him back. I had been continuing the war on my own since then. I was getting close to the vampire known as Shawl once again. He was tricky, and not above setting an ambush. The latest information I had received from one of his soldiers (before I killed him) made me think I was heading for a possible ambush once again. But I was going anyway. I hated Shawl. And hopefully I had at least one trick of my own up my sleeve. The information led me to a deserted town where a few buildings were still standing. I wasn't there for long before I was attacked.

The silent vampire that scratched me from behind was named Dron. We had fought to a standstill a month ago before he took off into the night. Now he was back. But he should have brought a stake. I did. Mine was in a mini-crossbow. Small enough that he didn't see it from behind me. When he got in front of me, he hissed. He also spied the crossbow, but too late. I'd already fired the wooden bolt at him. I hit him where I'd aimed, right in his heart. Dron was taken off the board. Two more vampires jumped out of the darkness, clawing at me. They knocked my crossbow away, but it was empty anyway. I did however have an extra stake up my sleeve. An old habit of mine. This one found another vampire's heart. That was two down. The last one had a gun! He shot me in the right shoulder before I could dodge. He had loaded the gun with a silver bullet. It wouldn't kill me, but it did sting. I fell and could not immediately rise to my feet. I then found out that he had more than one bullet in the gun.

The unknown vampire fired again and hit me in the chest. More silver in me. This wasn't looking good. Then it got worse. Shawl walked out from the shadows to greet me.
"It's been a good game, Victor. But I'm tired of running. It's finally time for you to die." Shawl was walking with a cane. But not because he needed it. The cane was made of wood, and one end was sharpened. It was a weapon, one that could finish me. He raised it up above me while the other vampire held me down.
"Any last words", continued Shawl, "before I win this final battle?"
"Just...this", I gasped. "I didn't come here alone." Shawl had thought that my partner, Randall, had been killed. But Randall was alive and coming out of the shadows behind Shawl. I think he finally smelled him, but it was too late. Randall roared like a lion and delivered the killing blow to Shawl from behind him, with his own wooden stake. To his credit, even though he struck

Shawl from that angle in the darkness, he didn't miss. It was a good strike. It made me proud that he was my partner.

"Randall", said Shawl. "I thought I killed you. That was...a good one. Bravo, Victor. Looks like you win...after all." Those were his final words. I was glad to see that one die. But the battle wasn't over. I finally regained enough strength to throw the vampire who had been holding me. But we were out of stakes! Or not, as Randall proved by pulling the small one out of Dron's body. Five minutes had passed since Dron died, so he wasn't coming back even with the stake removed from him. This time I held the vampire, and Randall threw the stake. He didn't want to waste any time. But the stake missed his heart, if only slightly. I wasn't strong enough to hold him, and he broke free. Randall wasn't done fighting yet. He had grabbed a large rock, and he used it to cave in part of the evil vampire's skull. That was quite a sight. Randall then pulled the stake out of the vampire's chest, and this time put it where it belonged. That shot to the heart did the trick. I watched him drop, but was more interested in seeing Shawl's lifeless body. Randall and I both stood over him. There wasn't much left to say. But I said it anyway.
"Finally. We finally got you, you bastard. I hope you rot right here." Randall and I walked off, leaving him there. He wasn't coming back to life. That part of our war was finally over. America won it's war soon after that. All in all, 1945 turned out to be a pretty good year.

-The End-

The Truce Ends

The year was 1948. The ongoing war between vampire factions had come to an unofficial truce. The ones who had previously wanted to destroy or enslave humans had for the most part stopped what they were doing. Now they were just existing, much like those of us who pretty much left the humans alone. Every now and then we would feed, but we'd try to feed on the most corrupt people we could find. Criminals, gangsters, that sort. And so, vampire activity had come to an all time low. At least since I'd become one in 1929. My partner Randall had killed one of my worst enemies, Roderick Shawl. My former master, Steven Burns, was still out there somewhere. But I decided to abandon my search for him temporarily, as things were quite peaceful. Except for Randall. He was becoming more rebellious. I suppose it does happen. I was his supposed master, but I always treated him as an equal. That may have had something to do with it. One night when I awoke, he was simply gone. I thought he might be hunting, but two nights passed and he did not return.

I was afraid that Randall was trying to reignite the vampire war. He had been talking about it. How he missed the thrill he got from combat. Well, he had been a soldier before I bit him. I thought it was a bad idea, as I was finally content with the way things were. There was at least one friend of his that I could contact, so I went to see him. A vampire named Gar Harris shared our ideology; he talked to Randall nearly as often as I did. I was able to find Gar and ask him if he had heard from Randall. Gar told me that he had. And that Randall told him that he was going off in search of Steven by himself. That was bad news. When I asked Gar if he knew where Steven was, he gave me the name of a town nearby. It seemed to me that Steven had been watching us, as he would never be that easy to find otherwise. All of this sounded to me like a trap. And if it was, then Randall had just walked right into it. I went back home to get some things. Then I left to see if I could find my partner.

It's usually difficult to find a vampire that will take you right to Steven Burns. But when I arrived in town, that's exactly what I found. A vampire named Jerzi told me he would take me to him. Again, I smelled a trap. But I decided to go with him anyway. We arrived at an abandoned warehouse. I had Jerzi go in ahead of me. I sniffed around to see if I could detect Steven, or any other vampires. But all I smelled was death. And another familiar scent. It was Randall. I could see him, even in the dark, in a corner of the building. He was sitting motionless on the floor. With a wooden stake in his heart. I was too late.
"A present", said Jerzi, "from my master, Steven."
"You must have known that you would die after bringing me here", I replied.
"We all do what we must". I whirled around to strike hlm, but he jumped straight up onto a beam above us. But he wasn't going anywhere. I was angry and I was prepared for a fight.

I leapt up and struck the beam with both hands. I hit it with enough force to break it and send Jerzi back to the floor. He hissed at me once. Then his self-preservation must have kicked in, as he headed for the exit. Since my partner had once been a soldier, we had grenades back

19

at our place. I had brought one with me, and now was the time to use it. I pulled the pin and threw it over Jerzi's head. It continued past him to the doorway. He was cut off and knew it, so he turned around. But he was too late to escape the explosion. It blasted the front of the warehouse to pieces. It also shredded Jerzi pretty good. He was thrown towards me and landed at my feet. He looked bad, but he was still alive. Not for long; I had also brought a stake with me. I quickly put it through the creature's heart, putting him out of his misery. I then walked over to Randall and picked him up. This was not the first partner I'd lost in this war. I was about to take him back to our graveyard for burial. Then I realized that Steven may have been watching me. If so, I had a message for him.

"Steven! Lets finish this, just you and I. It has to end, one way or the other. Soon". I then went back home to bury Randall and think about how I would destroy my greatest enemy.

THE END.

The Blade of Vengeance

In 1949 I was still hot on the trail of my former master and enemy, Steven Burns. I'm a vampire named Victor and I usually work alone. I tried working with partners in the past in my war on evil vampires, but they died on me. So I wasn't looking for a new one. However, I did find a temporary one in a most interesting human named Brandon. He was a vampire hunter as well, and had somehow heard of me. He sought me out and I allowed him to find me. We had a conversation. He had a very unusual story. He told me that he was shot and killed in World War Two. But his death was only temporary. When I asked how this was, he told me a story. After he died, he had a talk with his dead uncle. Brandon's uncle told him that his body was still clinging to life and that he would be sent back to Earth to take on a new mission. Brandon was shown a special knife called the 'Blade of Vengeance'. It was a tool forged by monks over a century ago. It's only purpose was to kill vampires. His uncle handed him the knife and told him how it worked. After that, Brandon came back to life. It was quite a tale, one I'm not sure I believed at the time.

I was hunting a vampire named Calculex, so I allowed Brandon to tag along. Don't ask where these vampires came up with these odd names. I had fought ones named Dron, Jerzi and Vrax, and was used to their eccentricities. Besides, I was hunting a vampire next to a man who had died and come back with a knife and a mission. My life was anything but predictable.

"Explain to me again", I whispered, "just how this blade of yours works."

"I told you", Brandon answered", "it's odd. When I see a vampire, it just appears in my right hand. Like it did when I met you."

"I saw. That was weird. Where does the thing even come from?"

"Another dimension? Who knows. As long as it works. And I've used it before."

"How can a blade even kill a vampire?", I questioned. "I always thought it had to be a wooden stake."

"I don't know that either. But it can. This thing seeks vampires out and kills them. Almost on it's own."

"It didn't kill me when I met you."

"True", replied Brandon. "And when we find Calculex, you'll see why."

We were talking too loud. I should have known better by now. Calculex had heard us. He jumped down from where he was perched in a tree. That old trick. His fingernails were like claws when he raked my back with them on the way down. I fell, and before I could react, he kicked me in the face. I was temporarily out of it, so he turned his attention to my newest partner.

"A human", Calculex said. "I can smell it. Fresh blood. Thank you Victor, for bringing me a snack." The blade had already appeared in Brandon's right hand.

"Snack on this", he said. He threw the blade at Calculex. But too slowly; the vampire caught the blade by the handle!

"If you fancy yourself a vampire slayer", chuckled Calculex, "you'll have to do better than that. A nice weapon you've given me. Wait...what is this?" Calculex's hand that was holding the blade was now pointing it at his heart. And it was moving closer to him. He used his one hand to hold the other, but that only slowed it down. It was eerie, watching it inch closer to him. He told the blade to stop, but it wasn't listening. It was quite a struggle he put up, but in the end, the blade made one final thrust that he could not halt. The blade pierced his heart, and the vampire dropped dead.

I had recovered from the beast's savage attack by this time. I walked over to Calculex's body. But I didn't dare touch that blade.

"You see", explained Brandon. "I'm only the keeper of the blade. It's host or whatever. But if you put that blade in the hands of a vampire it'll kill him. Which is why it never tried to kill you. And yeah, don't grab it. As far as I know, there's no stopping it until it does what it has to.

Then it simply disappears."

"Good advice. I've never heard of anything quite like that. It borders on the supernatural. Then again, so do I." I watched the blade, and sure enough, it faded slowly from this plane. To where I don't know, nor do I want to. But one thing was clear. Brandon's story was true. The knife worked just like he said it would. I thanked him for his help on this mission. We both decided to go our own separate ways as we felt that we worked best alone. Besides, that guy didn't need a babysitter. Still, I hoped that our paths would cross again. We were, after all, working towards the same goal. He was trying to end this war, and so was I. By any means necessary.

-THE END-

Rivalry

I had finally caught up to Steven Burns, my former vampire master, in 1949. Don't ask me how I did, I'm not really sure. It's almost like he let me find him. That is a possibility. My name is Victor, and I was turned into a vampire by Burns back in 1929. After twenty years we were finally going to have it out. He started by telling me he was disgusted by the way I behaved as a vampire. A 'human-lover', he called me. I told him I was disgusted by his smell. I then tried to surprise him with my speed. I jumped at him, but he somehow caught me. By my throat! He hadn't lost any speed. He threw me thirty feet into a tree. I got up and he was coming at me. He seemed to be holding something behind his back in the darkness. I pulled out my wooden stake and waited for him. He must have anticipated me bringing a stake. He was holding something all right. It was a sword! He sliced the stake in half before I could pull it away. My stake was sliced too cleanly to still be used as a weapon, so I dropped it.

Now Burns was swinging the sword at me. I didn't even know he owned one. I was doing a good job of dodging it so far. He finally managed to slice my left shoulder, but just barely. That didn't slow me down.
"I'm sorry", he said, "That I ever created you. You've been nothing but trouble since day one."
"you've been no better. Do you even know how many lives you have destroyed?"
"I must confess, I don't. Nor do I particularly care. I do what I must to survive."
"That's a lie", I continued. "I only do what I do because you turned me into this. I feed when I have to, but you...you crossed a line a long time ago. And now I'm going to see that you pay."
"Ha", was his response. "I'll die when it's my time. And that is not today." He kept coming at me with that darn sword. He even took some of my hair with it. At this point I was wishing that I still had a partner. But Steven had made sure that I was alone in this battle.

As we fought, if you can call it that, Steven's face

contorted. He looked less human than I remembered. Of course, he wasn't human anyway. But his ears and his fangs elongated. And his skin even changed color. He was starting to look light blue. More like a Nosferatu, or 'homo-vampiri', as he liked to say. My reaction was to grow my fangs and claws. We circled and growled at each other like animals. I still liked to think of myself as human. But you wouldn't know it if you had seen me just then. He was swinging wildly with the sword, so I managed to get in a kick to his ribs. Which made him growl louder. I came back to my senses somewhat, and remembered that I had brought a grenade with me to finish him off. I took it out of what was left of my coat. I even showed it to him. I made the mistake of looking at it when I pulled the pin. Burns took advantage of my momentary distraction and swung his sword. This time it connected with me...and took my right hand off!

I howled in pain, but somehow did not forget that there was now a live grenade on the ground. I leapt away as far as I could, which was not far now. Steven almost forgot to move, too. He finally jumped in another direction, but too late to avoid all of the fragments of the exploding grenade. The concussive force of the grenade finally separated him from his sword. I walked over to where he was, and stood between him and the sword. His back was bleeding. So he did get hit by some shrapnel after all.

"You're in no shape", he hissed, "to continue this battle."
"Neither are you, Steven." I tried to sound tough, but it was getting difficult to remain conscious. Fortunately, someone else had just shown up.

The new arrival must have been watching our battle in the dark. It was Gar, a vampire friend of mine. Steven was on his feet again, and looking at the two of us.

"Very well then, Victor", Steven said. "We'll finish this some other time." With that, he turned and leapt away; too far for me to follow even if I wanted to. I was already using shape-shifting techniques to heal my hand. It would regenerate in time. I thanked Gar for his timely arrival. But as weak as I was, I still had a warning for Steven, if he could still hear me.

"Get used to looking over your shoulder." After that, Gar walked me home. I didn't win, but I survived. My war would be still be waiting for me when I was better.

- THE END –

The Werewolf

By 1951 I'd almost forgotten that I once lost a hand to Steven Burns, my greatest enemy. Almost, but not quite. Fortunately it had long since grown back. One of the perks of being a vampire. My name is Victor Vanashez and I usually worked alone. But not always. There was a vampire I knew named Gar who had somehow managed to stay alive. So I worked with him sometimes. And a normal human named Brandon Vale who was actually anything but normal. He had a supernatural ability to summon a vampire-killing blade that I didn't quite understand. At that point in time, those were really the only two friends I had left. I didn't know at the time if I'd ever find anymore. A vampire's life can be a lonely one. But not always. While I didn't make any friends that year, I did dispose of a few enemies. So that was a good thing. It wasn't until the next year that I did find another friend.

In the summer of 1952 I was hunting one of enemies. A vampire named Hill. At least I thought I was hunting him. It was dark and foggy that night. The fog was messing with my enhanced senses. I followed Hill for some time, but then lost him. He somehow got behind me. So I guessed that he knew I was tailing him. Especially when a rather large rock hit me in the back.

"Stay away from me, Vanashez", he yelled. "Or you'll get more of the same." I was still trying to rise after that strike when I heard a growl. But it wasn't coming from Hill. It came from a different direction. And it did not sound like a noise a vampire would make. I certainly never heard it before. Then again, I'd never encountered a werewolf before. Even with the fog, I could see the beast. It wasn't even a vampire disguised as a wolf, I could tell. This thing was huge and standing on two legs. It seemed odd to me that it was wearing blue shorts. Then again, werewolves do turn back into people, so it sort of made sense. I think they can only come out during the three nights of the full moon. And this was the third night. I didn't know much else about them, but I didn't have a lot of time for questions just then.

The werewolf saw me, but he sniffed the air and looked past me at Hill. Hill was as shocked as I was. Maybe he did not believe in werewolves. The beast just snarled and kept watching us both. So I decided to introduce myself.

"My name is Victor. Do you have a name? Or can you speak when you're all wolf-like?"

"Bart", it shouted back. At first I thought he barked. Then I realized that he was trying to speak.

"Bart", I continued. "Good. Now, the vampire over there

is named Hill. He's the bad guy. I like people. And werewolves. I think they're swell." I was trying to remain calm and not show this creature any fear. I thought it might help. Hill's thinking was different than mine.

"You've lost it, Victor. Just kill the thing and let's get back to what we were doing". I thought that was rather impolite. Apparently, so did Bart. He howled at the night sky and perhaps the moon. He then attacked Hill quickly. He covered several yards with one leap. I'd seen vampires do this, but not at that speed. He lashed out at Hill with his claws. Hill grew claws of his own and went on the offensive.

It wasn't the way I'd planned things, but as far as distractions go, a werewolf was a good one. So I pulled out my wooden stake and watched the two of them go at it. Hill lost his left ear to Bart's wild and unstoppable clawing. Bart's left shoulder got cut pretty deep by Hill's now-ridiculously long claws. They were both getting sliced up pretty good. But I only wanted Hill dead. Neither one was watching me, so I came up behind Bart and tossed him aside, as heavy as he was. As a vampire, I can lift over half a ton. Throwing a giant furball wasn't really that difficult. Hill looked surprise by the reprieve.

"Don't thank me just yet", I said. He never saw the stake in my hand, as he was focused on surviving his latest battle. But he did look down and see it when it went into his heart. He howled in pain and disappointment. And that was it for the vampire named Hill. I just hoped that Bart understood why I tossed him aside.

Bart was back on his feet and still growling. It was as if he had seen what happened, but was still trying to make sense of it all. I think he finally got it. He stopped growling and stood there looking at me. Then he dropped to the ground. I wondered why; I hadn't thrown him that hard. I stepped closer and saw something amazing happen. Bart was transforming back into a human. That was something to see. He lost almost all of his hair, and some height too. At least his shorts managed to stay on.

"Thanks", he said. "I take it you're one of the good vampires? I've heard of some like you. Not many, but a few anyway."

"I like to think so. You're the first werewolf I've ever met. And I have to say, it's a pleasure."

"Ha. I don't hear that very often. Not since I was cursed, anyway."

"I know the feeling", I responded. We talked some more after that introduction. I told him how I was bitten in 1929 and had become a vampire. He told me he was bitten and scratched by a werewolf two years ago. He wasn't even sure which injury changed him. But he did know that a silver bullet could kill him. As strong as we both were, we all have our weaknesses. Maybe that's why I decided to keep him around. Unlikely as it was, I had made a new friend. Life wasn't so lonely after all.

-THE END-

The Link

It was 1953 and I was on the trail of an evil vampire. His name was Link. My name is Victor. I'd been a vampire myself since 1929. The one who turned me was named Steven Burns. We'd clashed a few times since, with neither one of us gaining a decisive victory. I had learned that Link worked for Steven. I figured on taking out another one of his soldiers. Possibly more, if Link wasn't alone. But he was a scout and usually hunted alone. I used to be like that but had realized the value of having friends. One of my new friends was Bart. He understood my curse as he had one of his own. Bart had lycanthropy, which meant he was cursed to change into a wolf-man or werewolf under the full moon. I asked Bart if he wished to accompany me on my search for Link.

"What's the date?", Bart asked me.

"Thursday. February the 12th", I responded.

"Okay. The moon will be full tomorrow night. I won't change until then."

"All right", I replied. "Tomorrow night it is."

We waited until Bart transformed into a six and a half foot tall werewolf on Friday the 13th to go out looking for Link. He was only six foot one before the change. I did ask him where the extra mass came from, but he wasn't sure. He joked that perhaps it came from another dimension. I figured that it had more to do with a metamorphic change to his skeletal and muscular systems. But I had not done much research on werewolves. During the conversation, he asked where I got my vampiric strength from. I didn't fully know, but some of the knowledge was in my brain since Steven had bitten me.

"I think", I said, "that it has a lot to do with my blood type. I was once type AB, but all vampires are type V. Our blood changes once we're bitten. Sort of a transfer from the host vampire. It infects and changes human blood into type V, which stimulates the adrenal glands to a higher extent than a human's. Which allows our muscles to do more than they ever could before the change." I was saying the words, but only partially understanding them. Some of the information that was in my brain came from Steven. Bart didn't really seem too interested in my big words; he was growling softly and sniffing the air for any scent that wasn't human or animal.

"Also", I continued, "vampires have hollow bones, like a bird's. They allow us to fly if we feel inclined to shape-shift some of our mass into giant wings. I've tried it, but I don't really have the balance for it yet." Bart stopped and looked at me. At first I thought I was annoying him. Then I saw his nose twitching. He'd found something...or someone. I focused my own enhanced senses. Sure enough, there was the scent of a vampire on the wind. Bart's wolf-nose had picked up on it first. He was turning out to be a good partner. We were in such a position that Link couldn't detect us. We silently walked further and saw him. He was feeding on a rabbit he'd caught. Another reason he did not know we were there. I figured we'd keep up the silent approach. However, since it was the first night of the full moon, Bart had another idea. He howled and leapt at Link. So much for the element of surprise.

Link turned around and saw Bart coming at him. He quickly fell backwards to allow Bart's momentum to take him past Link. Bart quickly recovered and went back after the vampire. Link looked shocked to see an actual werewolf. Just like I was the first time I saw Bart. Maybe werewolves are more rare than vampires. In any event, the two were now engaged in battle. Clawing at each other, seeing who could inflict the most damage. That didn't get either of them too far, so Link tried another tactic. With his great strength, he shoved Bart a few yards back into a tree. He then turned and began to run.

31

He was trying to escape a werewolf, but did not know that I was there. He was almost on top of me when I spoke.

"Going somewhere?", I asked. My voice startled him as he had been so busy with his fight that he never detected my presence. But he didn't stop in time. I was able to get my left hand around his throat. I originally wanted to question him on Steven's current location, but a bloodlust had begun to rise in me as I watched the battle. I had my right hand drawn back and was holding a wooden stake. So I thrust it forward before Link had a chance to get out of my grasp. I managed to get the stake through his heart, and that was it for Link. That made Bart happy. We hadn't gotten any new information on Steven Burns, but we did eliminate an evil vampire scout. And as Bart put it, 'we had fun doing it'. So we did end up having a productive Friday the 13th.

-The End.

The Grand Metamorphosis

In 1955 I decided to try something I hadn't attempted before. My name is Victor. I'm a vampire. I had a friend who was a werewolf. Most days of the year, he was regular Bart Stanton. But for three nights every month he'd become a werewolf. Such was his curse. This change intrigued me. Since vampires are shape-shifters,

I wondered if I could become a realistic looking werewolf. So one month, I waited for the full moon. Bart went through his metamorphosis and decided to go and see what kind of trouble he could get into. I stayed behind at the mausoleum we lived in. Vampires are usually pretty strong under the full moon, so I figured that might make what I was attempting easier. I started with the easy stuff. I already knew I could elongate my fangs and fingers, so I did that. A vampire has a great deal of control over their muscular system. Changing the shape of bones is more difficult. But I found that if I thought about it, I could extend my jaw and nose outward. I was already looking more wolfish. The next part did hurt a little bit. I extended my spinal column to grow an inch. I also enlarged my hands.

Things were going pretty well. I was also able to lengthen my ears some. Then came the tricky part. I needed my hair to grow...but all over my body. I'll admit, that one stung! It was more like a burning sensation, shooting hairs out of their follicles at a great speed. But it worked! From what I could see, I made a pretty convincing werewolf. I already knew how to howl, but I tried it anyway. That sounded good as well. But it may have been going too far. Because that howl was heard by Bart, who was already on his way back from a successful rabbit-hunt. Well, he had to eat. And he did love to hunt. Unfortunately, he was back a little early. I guess I should have told him ahead of time what I was planning on doing. He threw the door open and did not recognize me. Then he gave me a combat-growl; that I recognized.

"Where is Victor?", he asked. "I can smell him; I know he's here." Good thing for me I could still speak in this form.

"Bart", I yelled. "It's me. You can smell me because I'm

right here. I was...trying something new. How do you like it?" He just stood there for several seconds, sniffing me.

"Victor", he answered. "You are one strange vampire. Still, having this power could be useful in the future." I agreed. Then I started the process of shifting back to normal. That hurt more than the first time! That was a rather interesting night, but it would be a little while before I'd try that again.

It was 1956 when I tried turning myself into a werewolf again. I'm a vampire, but being a shape-shifter, I can also resemble a werewolf. Like my friend, Bart, who actually is one. We were looking for a vampire named Perez, who was a loyal servant of my former master, Steven Burns. I'd heard that Perez was in my town and wondered if it was a coincidence. Whether it was or not, I decided to disguise myself while Bart and I went hunting for him. Just two werewolves looking for a vampire. And we found him. I caught his scent as he was leaving a tavern. Bart and I followed him. We could both see pretty well in the dark, but it was getting harder to keep him in sight. That meant he must have known he was being followed. He did; when we rounded a corner, he was waiting behind a boulder to ambush whoever was tailing him. He was surprised to see two werewolves there.

"What do you want with me?", he asked.

"Where is Steven?", I replied. "Is he with you?"

"He's not here", he answered. "I came to this town to recruit vampires for him. But why do two werewolves want to know? He has nothing to do with your kind."

"I understand if you can't see through my disguise", I said. "It's me, Victor Vanashez. And I don't take kindly to recruiting in my town."

"That scent", Perez answered. "It is you!" He started to

lean forward as if to attack, but must have thought better of it. Instead, he turned and leapt twenty feet away. Not to be outdone, Bart jumped just as far. I decided to run and allow Bart some time to take Perez down. Bart did catch him, and they were wrestling on the ground. For a few seconds. Suddenly, Perez threw Bart several feet away. Since he was clear, I decided to jump in. I pulled out my concealed wooden stake and leapt on top of Perez before he could get up. I had aimed it for his heart, but he caught my wrist on the way down!

Perez was a strong one, to throw Bart as he had from his position on the ground. And now he had stopped me from killing him. But only temporarily. Bart jumped back into the fray. And when I say jumped, I mean he jumped up and landed on my hand that was holding the stake! His weight brought the stake down, and through Perez's heart. Since Bart weighed over 275 pounds in his wolf-form, that didn't do my hand any good. But I would heal. Perez would not. I made sure he was dead before I climbed off of him.

"Sorry about that, partner", said Bart. "It was the quickest way I could think of to finish him off."

"It's okay, I can heal this pretty fast. I think some bones are bruised, but nothing broken. It's worth it, to have killed another member of Burns' crew. Thanks for the assist. But now we're going to have to move to another town again."

"That's fine with me", Bart replied. "Werewolves are nomads anyway. Speaking of which...you really need to change back. That disguise might fool a vampire or a human, but a werewolf would see right through it." I agreed and we laughed about it. I think it was the last time I disguised myself as a werewolf. It worked well enough, but the transformations hurt, and that disguise wasn't really as effective as I'd hoped it would be. You live and learn, I suppose.

-The End.

Not Quite Human

Things had been quiet for awhile in my never-ending battle against vampires. I'm Victor Vanashez, and I'm a vampire myself. But not the human-hating kind. I'd be happy just to co-exist with people, since I was only human myself once. When I was bitten in 1929, I never really turned evil. I was 29 then and I'm 61 now, but I still try to see things the way I used to. But, since sunlight is like poison to me, I only go out at night. I still talked to people sometimes. They can't really tell that I'm a vampire. I disguise it pretty well. I usually moved from town to town pretty quickly, but this one time I had settled down for longer than usual. Like, months longer. I had a few aquaintances I'd see often in the bars at night. I was even becoming more optimistic in my view of life. I should have known it was too good to last.

I was in my favorite bar one night in 1961. Even my favorite waitress, Summer, was there. I'll admit, the place had become a nice distraction from hunting vampires. But just because I'd stopped hunting them, it didn't mean they'd gone away for good.

A stranger dressed in black walked into the bar that night. I didn't pay any attention to him at first. But minutes later I did catch his scent. He was an evil vampire named Sloan. I hadn't seen him in two years, and he'd grown a beard. But I still recognized him. I didn't want any trouble inside the bar, so I paid my bill and headed for the door. But Sloan always was a troublemaker. He got up and blocked my way to the door.

"Sloan", I said. "Not here."

"Why not? You gone soft? Or maybe these people mean something to you. Maybe I'll just pick one and see for myself." I was trying to contain my anger, but it didn't work. He was in front of the doorway, so I pushed him outside...about fifteen feet. The people in the bar seemed shocked by my behavior. But at least they didn't see how far I'd pushed Sloan.

"Stay inside", I warned them.

I went outside and Sloan was already on his feet.

"You broke my sunglasses", he said. "That'll cost you."

"You know what? I'm just going to let you leave. Get out of town and don't come back. I won't even come after you."

"Well", he replied, "that's not going to happen. Steven still wants you dead or working for him. So what's it gonna be?" He meant Steven Burns, the vampire who turned me. But there was no way I'd ever work for him.

"I'm done with Steven", I said. "And I'm done with you." I quickly grabbed Sloan and picked him up. I then hurled him into the side of a tree ten feet away. He shook his head and got back up before I could reach him. I was about to hit him, but he grabbed my arm.

"You're done, all right", he said. He then threw me up into the tree. I broke a few branches on the way up. But I landed on one on the way down. He hissed at me and motioned for me to come down.

I swung my feet into Sloan's face while holding onto the branch. I then landed in back of him. He got up and turned towards me, but too slowly. I'd already gotten the concealed wooden stake out of my sleeve. He hit me, but didn't see the stake. I made a left feint toward his jaw, but he blocked it easily. Of course, I only did that to keep his attention off the stake in my right hand. With my next move, I sunk that into his heart.

"You...you sneaky little...", was all he got out. Then he dropped dead at my feet. I was glad at first. Then I looked up. I finally realized that the patrons of the bar had seen the whole thing. In my anger, I had forgotten where we were. They were all looking at me like I was some monster from the movies. Like what they'd seen couldn't be real. But it was, and they knew it. There was no way I could explain this so that they would accept me. I knew my time in that nice little town was done.

"I'm sorry", was all I could think to say to them. Then I ran off into the woods. I learned something that day. I had to stop playing human and accept who I was. For their sake and for mine. Even though I despised vampires, I was still one of them. And nothing would ever change that harsh reality.

-The End-

Vampire Vs. Mummy

Seems like I'm always moving from town to town. And living in a cemetery. But, being a vampire, that's not so unusual. I had found a quiet cemetery to stay at in 1966. One night, I was out for a long time. Checking out the new town, stuff like that. I even found a hog in the woods to feed on. It had been a pretty good night, and I was headed back home to sleep. But when I got closer to my home, I saw two new coffins that were not there when I left. Had someone moved in? I could see that they were both empty. One was pretty standard, but the other one

38

looked...Egyptian? It looked like something you'd store a mummy in. Then I began to detect some odd scents. I couldn't place the first one, but the second one was a vampire. I sniffed the air some more and determined that it was a vampire I'd met before. Named Voz. He was a slippery character and had managed to get away from me twice before. I figured he was there looking for revenge.

"Voz", I said. "I can smell you out there." But there was no answer.

I walked in the direction of his scent, and caught the other one again. Like something dead, but with a smell I'd never encountered before. So I decided to be cautious. I had also remembered that Voz liked using swords. I had to find him before he found me. It was then that Voz chose to speak.

"Ledda...mumi...lif", he said. It sounded like chanting. And there was something familiar about it...in the memories that I had gained from Steven Burns when he bit me. It took a few seconds, but I realized that it was a chant to allow a mummy to return to life. So there was one here! I didn't like that idea, as I'd never gone up against one before. At least hearing Voz speak gave away his position. He was sitting on top of a mausoleum. I could see him up there in the moonlight.

"Ledda...mumi...lif", he said for the second time. I recalled at that point that the chant had to be spoken twice. So now the mummy would most likely be active, if the chant worked. I looked around me, and sure enough, there was a mummy coming towards me. And he was holding a sword.

"As you can see, Victor", said Voz, "I have found myself a mummy. Bad luck for you, old man."

"I can take him", I replied. "Then I'm coming for you."

"I rather doubt that. But we'll see." I tried to think of what a mummy's weakness would be. A cat? Too bad there were none around. I wished I had a sword, but of course I didn't. The mummy was moving faster than I thought he'd be able to. He swung that sword and nearly caught me with his first shot. I was distracted because I knew there was a chant to stop a mummy...I just couldn't remember what it was!

"He's going to get you", chided Voz. The mummy swung again and got even closer to striking me the second time. There were too many tombstones getting in my way. A third sword-strike came, but I was able to leap out of it's way this time. I needed to get that sword away from him.

"Careful, Victor", warned Voz. "You might just wind up dead!" I looked up to see Voz grinning from his perch. That proved to be a mistake. The mummy thrusted forward with the sword...and caught me. To the side of my mid-section. Which did not feel good at all. I howled, but took the opportunity to kick the mummy in the stomach. That caused him to let go of the sword. Which was still stuck in me.

"That does look painful", commented Voz. The mummy was now trying to hit the sword in order to drive it in deeper. Now I had to move around with a sword sticking out of me. My night was going from bad to worse. Until I finally remembered the chant!

"Lida Mumi dii, lida mumi dii", I chanted. The mummy froze where it was. Seconds later, it finally keeled over.

"Eh", said Voz. "What did you do? That was my mummy!"

"Hmm", I answered. "Then you'll really hate this next part.

With some effort, I pulled the sword out of myself. I

tried shape-shifting some to begin to heal the damage. Then I took the sword over to where the mummy was lying on the ground. I raised the sword over my head and brought it down. With enough force to chop the mummy's head off.

"He won't be coming back", I growled. "And neither will you, Voz." I looked up to the top of the mausoleum just in time to see Voz jump off the other side of it. I could hear him running away in the distance. I let him go, as I was too tired and sore from my battle. Plus, the sun was just about to rise. I left that area of the cemetery and made my way back home. With Voz's sword. I didn't get to kill him, but I did cost him a mummy and a sword. Not to mention a coffin or two. I figured someone would find the beheaded mummy. Maybe the police. But I didn't care, I just wanted to sleep and heal from my injury. My revenge against Voz would have to wait. But that's okay. After the events of that night, I figured I'd take care of him soon enough. He could run, but he could not hide. Not from me.

THE END.

Two Blades

In 1969 I caught up with the vampire, Voz, once again. The last time we had met, he used a mummy to do his fighting for him. This time, I'd heard that he was staying in a certain town in New York for a few days. He was planning on attending a festival of some kind. Woodstock, I believe they called it. But I found him days before it began. I met him one night in a wooded area. I was able to sniff him out with my enhanced senses. Problem is, Voz had the same senses. So he knew I was following him. And unfortunately for me, he was carrying a sword. He always liked those.

"Victor", he said. "So, we meet again. Too bad you didn't bring a sword. I assume you have a wooden stake tucked away somewhere? You're so predictable."

"Maybe", I replied. "But knowing that won't help you. This time I'm putting an end to you."

"Try it and see what happens."

We squared off in an opening in the woods. No full moon that night, but it didn't matter. We could both see pretty well in the dark. Voz growled once and came at me with the sword. He was quick with that thing. It nearly caught my right arm. In fact, he swung at it, but my concealed wooden stake stopped his blow. The stake was, however, cut in half.

"There goes your only weapon", said Voz. "Next time, it'll be your head." He swung for me again. And missed. Luckily, I was able to grab his wrist this time. I had stopped his weapon from reaching me, but he still had one hand free. That's when my secret weapon stepped out from behind the trees. Voz saw him immediately.

"Meet my friend, Brandon", I said to Voz.

"I could smell him", said Voz. "But I assumed it was just

some human walking through these woods. But no matter, I see he only has a knife."

"Yeah", replied Brandon. "But I'm good with it."

Having said that, Brandon hurled the knife past me and at Voz. It nearly struck him, too. But the vampire was fast enough to catch the handle in the air. I knew what had to happen next, so I released Voz and stepped back.

"Ha", laughed Voz. "You're not as good as you think. Now I have two blades."

"True", replied Brandon. "But not for long." Brandon was known by some as 'The Blade of Vengeance'. It was because the knife he carried had supernatural powers. It had been twenty years since I saw it in action, but I remembered what it was capable of. It only appeared in his right hand when he saw a vampire. In this case, Voz. After it appeared, it sought out the vampire and would not stop until it killed him. Which was always a surprise to the vampire.

"What is this", said Voz, as the knife started inching toward his heart. He dropped his sword to hold his other hand back. But that would only work for so long. And the blades' power would not allow him to simply drop it.

"This can't happen", said Voz. "I'm the master of the edged weapon."

I had picked up the sword by that time. Voz was still struggling against the knife. But with one final thrust, it found it's target. The blade pierced Voz's heart. He cried out and fell to the ground. Brandon had assured me that the blade would be deadly to Voz. But I wasn't taking any chances with this one. Voz stopped twitching, but I decided to bring the sword down on him anyway. I cut his head off just to make sure he would not bother me anymore. The blade disappeared, as it always did when its mission was complete. Brandon was just looking at me.

"What", I said. "You can't be too careful with an evil vampire." He laughed at that statement.

We talked a little after that. Brandon was now in his 40's, and thinking about retiring. He just wasn't sure how, since that knife would appear whenever he met a vampire. I wished him luck as we parted ways. I also told him that my own war against the evil vampires would likely only end with my death. We seemed to be two tragic pieces on a chess board. I wasn't sure if either of us could ever claim victory. But I knew that while I lived, I would never concede the game.

The End.

Meeting the Beast

In 1974 I heard some rather distressing news. My old friend and sometimes partner, Bart, had been killed by one of his own kind. He was a werewolf, and together we had defeated several vampires. He never even minded that I was a vampire myself. Another old friend of mine, a vampire named Gar, gave me the news. He even knew the name of Bart's assassin. A wolf man named Alex Frell. It took awhile to find Frell, as I had limited dealings with werewolves. But in 1976 I was able to track him down. He was staying in a barn in an otherwise deserted area. I thought I might have difficulty in getting to the barn undetected, what with Frell's sense of smell. So I didn't bother being sneaky. I suppose I could have waited until after that 3rd night of the full moon to attack. But no, I just wanted to see him pay. He transformed under the moon that night. By then, I was already within fifty feet of his place. I'm sure he knew I was coming, but I didn't care. I felt as if I'd prepared for him.

When I got to the front door, I knocked. Hard enough for the door to swing open. The wolf was waiting for me, as I figured.
"Fool", he said. "To think you could sneak up on me under the full moon? I could smell you...and I smelled a vampire. Correct?"
"Yes", I answered. "I'm a vampire. My name is Victor."
"Ah, I think I have heard of you. You kill your own kind."
"So do you", I said. "Remember Bart? He was a friend of mine."
"I see. You want revenge then. Sorry to disappoint you."
Frell actually leapt in the opposite direction. I guess he had heard of me. If so, he knew I was a survivor, and not to be messed with. But as I said, I came prepared. I saved a grenade from world war two. I had it with me, so I pulled the pin and threw it. Frell looked back to see what I was doing. I think his plan was to punch through the back wall. When he saw the grenade, he jumped at the wall. The grenade went off and blasted him through.

"That should do it", I said.
"Not quite", he responded. Frell had shrapnel in him, but was still getting up. We growled at each other, and I reached around behind me.

45

"If you're reaching for a wooden stake", he said, "that won't work on me."

"I know. I brought a gun. Just for you."

"A gun", he scoffed. "I see. Well, unless it has a silver bullet, I'm gonna grab some of this broken wood and put it in your chest."

"You'd be surprised at some of the fun stuff I've collected", I answered. I then aimed the gun at him and shot him in the chest. With a silver bullet. The last one I had, but one was all I'd need.

"I can't believe you did that", said Frell. "You did get your revenge. It won't bring him back, you know."

"True. But at least the world will be rid of you." Which is true, since the silver bullet did indeed kill the beast. I think it was then that I realized that despite what I was doing with my life, I wasn't quite a hero. Then again, I never told anyone I was. I was just doing what came naturally to me. Problem is, I was starting to like it just a little too much.

The End.

The Vampire Hunters

In 1980 I was working with the only partner I had left. I was 80 years old, and Gar was still alive. No one had put a wooden stake through either of us yet, despite our being vampires. The world had changed so much since I was bitten in 1929. It's a good thing I had a fake I.D. made years before, when it was easier. I had to keep changing the age on the darn thing, since vampires age slowly. I looked like I was 50, not 80. The war among vampires had all but faded as there were now far less of us left to roam the world. I was still looking for my former master, Steven Burns. But no luck; he had disappeared with most of the other evil vampires. Or he was hiding, since I wanted him dead. Gar and I still did things much the same way we had for years. When we would actually find a vampire and successfully exterminate him, we would take whatever money they had. Since we didn't have jobs, it was the only way we'd have any money. Gar would even steal from humans sometimes, but I never really got into that. Unless I determined that they were evil and had to die. Then I would eliminate them from society and take their money. I had to feed, and I could always spend the money when I went out at night.

But this lifestyle was beginning to become less than thrilling as the years rolled by. Since I did not work, I'd been spending other vampires' money pretty steadily since the 1950's. It became a habit and I never gave it much thought. Gar and I would go from town to town and frequent bars at night. They were open, and we still liked to be around people. We would drink, but our vampire metabolism basically immunized us from the effects of alcohol. Other than shopping, it was the only time we would actually interact with humanity. I always figured it was an attempt to hold onto what little humanity I felt I had left. I could feel a change in myself. I was starting to become more animalistic as the decades flew past. So I sat next to humans and tried to remember what life was like before I was turned into the monster I had become. It seemed to work for awhile. Until 1984, when Gar ran into a pair of vampire-hunters.

I had heard of them. Humans who hunted vampires in order to eradicate our presence from the world. One of the reasons so many of us had gone underground. I wasn't there in time to see it happen, but they are the ones who killed Gar.

Gar and I had split up that night to hunt. If we found any criminals that night, we agreed that we would relieve society of the burden they caused. I found no crimes being perpetrated that night, so I headed to our usual meeting spot. It was a dead-end alley in the center of town. But I never got there. Neither did Gar. I heard a cry that I thought was his voice, two blocks shy of our alley. I went to investigate and found two people there. And Gar, lying on his back. The humans had put a stake through his heart! From what I could piece together, they must have staged a mugging. One of them 'attacked' the other. When Gar showed up, they had fought and killed him. I don't know if they had been attempting to lure in a vampire, but that's what they got. And they were prepared for one. I just hoped they were not ready for another one so soon.

"Mike", yelled one of them. "I think we got another one!"

"Yeah, Joe", said the other. "I see him." I could see and smell the blood from Mike's nose. Gar had apparently broken it. Good, that means he put up a fight. Now all I had to do was finish it for him.

Mike raised a crossbow in front of him. I looked around and hastily grabbed a trash can lid. I got it in front of me just in time for it to catch the wooden bolt that was fired at me. Well, it caught most of it. Part of it went through the lid and hit my arm. Which caused me to growl and elongate my fangs. And my fingernails into claws. I was losing control again. This was happening more and more in that decade. I felt a sudden sadness. At my obvious loss of humanity, and Gar's death.

"You know what", I said. "Just go. Before I change my mind and tear both of you apart slowly."

"Mike", said Joe. "Come on, man. We're out of stakes. He's letting us go. Man, come on."

"Okay", replied Mike. "But this ain't over. A vampire killed my sister. Before I killed him. I ain't stopping til every last one of you freaks is dead."

I kept growling and slowly advancing to make sure they got the hint. They finally decided to take off. I knelt down to say good-bye to Garfield Harris. He was older than me, but somehow seemed always able to keep his animal instincts under control. I never did learn how. I knew I was losing it, and Gar's death didn't help matters. I now had the scent of the two hunters. I could find them if I wanted to. I was sad but somewhat calm for the moment. I knew that wouldn't last. I took Gar to the cemetery we had been living in and buried him there. Before I went to sleep, I hoped that Gar would be the last partner I would ever lose. I also I vowed to hunt and kill one or both of Gar's killers. My need for vengeance outweighed any pity I had previously felt for them.

The End.

One Last Chance

My name is Victor Vanashez. Since my last partner, Gar, had died, I made a decision to hunt down those responsible for his death. In 1986 I found one of them again. Since I was a vampire, I'd memorized his scent. Neither one of us had gone many miles since Gar died two years before. The vampire-hunters names were Joe and Mike. But when I caught up with Mike, he was alone. Perhaps his partner had abandoned him. Joe didn't seem to be into this lifestyle as much as Mike obviously was. Mike told me before that his sister was killed by a vampire. So I understood his motivation for going after them. But Gar was not an evil vampire. He was just trying to get by in his cursed life. And Mike had killed him. I still could not get too very angry with Mike; I certainly understood his point of view. But the animal in me still wanted to see him pay for Gar's death.

When I finally did find Mike, I watched him for one night. I was careful not to reveal my presence to him just yet. When he went out, he seemed like a normal person.

But when he went home...you should have seen his house. Plans and techniques for hunting vampires pinned to the walls. And multiple vampire-hunting weapons. I could see this stuff even from outside of his house. It looked to me as if he was obsessed with the idea of destroying all vampires. I figured I'd never be able to reason with him. It was going to come down to one last fight. Ending with either his death or mine.

I waited until the next night to tell him I was around. He was heading home, but I certainly did not want to face him there. On the way, he kept glancing around him. He must have sensed that he was being hunted. So I leapt out of the shadows once no one was around. To tell him he was right.

"Hello, Mike", I said. He whirled around to meet me, crossbow in hand. He must have had it under his jacket. I could see two extra stakes on his belt. But I already knew this guy was serious. All I had was a brick in each hand. Mostly to scare him, but I thought I might need them for something else. I also had a stake hidden up my sleeve, but that was an old habit of mine. You never know when you'll need one.

"Do we know each other?", he asked.

"Yeah. Two years ago, you killed my friend. And I let you and Joe go. That was a mistake."

"I do remember you", he continued. "A vampire, showing mercy. That did surprise me. Joe has retired since then. He had no stomach for this business, I'll admit. I talked him into it in the first place. If you recall, a vampire killed my sister. Which makes them my enemies. It's more personal for me."

"For me as well. Since Gar was the last friend I had. I'm just trying to survive, I'm not evil. Think about it. Was it my fault that I was bitten?" That made him hesitate. It looked as if he was thinking about it.

"It doesn't matter", he answered. "I'm sure you've killed your share of people in your time."

"You're right. But they deserved it."

"I'm not here to argue with you, vampire. Goodbye." Having said that, he fired the wooden stake at me. I watched it as best as I could, in the darkness. All of my enhanced senses had been waiting for this. Before it got to me, I got one of the bricks up in time to shield myself. The stake shattered on impact, but so did the brick.

"Nice trick", said Mike. "But I have more where that came from." He had already loaded another wooden stake. He was fast. But I was a vampire. He shot the second stake, and I leapt over it, towards Mike. I landed in front of him and swung at him. Somehow, he actually ducked! He really was fast. And he held his last stake in his hand.

"I don't want to kill you", I told him. "This can be over, if you want."

"For me", he replied, "it will never be over. Not while freaks like you still live." He brought the wooden stake down towards my heart. But I still had the other brick. I stopped it with that. Then knocked the stake out of his hand with the brick. He then knocked the brick out of my hand. We traded a few punches, but he did not hit hard enough to stop a vampire. Still, he wouldn't stop. I could see that now. He was truly obsessed, and I knew a little something about that. We continued to fight for two minutes. I then pulled out my concealed weapon. I hit him in the chest with it, but not very deep. He fell to the ground with that impact, and I landed on top of him.

"So", he said. "Finish it." I almost didn't. But the fight had awakened my bloodlust. And all I could think of was Gar. I realized that I had no more ties to vampires. Or humans.

"Very well", I responded. "For Gar!" I hit the stake with both hands. That drove it through Mike's heart. I ended his hunting career, and his life. At least he was now free from his obsession. I was still angry with Steven Burns for turning me into this thing in the first place. So I decided that before I died, I would indeed finish him. Even if I needed one last partner to do it.

Almost The End...

Nothing Lasts Forever

My name is Franklin Neil Stein. I used to live and work with a vampire. That sounds strange, I'm sure, but it's true. Figures that would happen to someone named Frank N. Stein. It wasn't entirely my idea, but I didn't have much choice in the matter. But let me start at the very beginning.

Victor Vanashez was born in the year 1900. When he was older, he felt lucky that he was too young to fight in the first world war in 1914. But that kind of luck did not hold. He lost nearly everything in the stock market crash of 1929. He even took to living on the streets for a time. That is, until he was attacked by a vampire! He was living in New York City at the time, and did not even believe in such creatures. But that didn't mean that they did not exist. He was 'turned' by a vampire master named Steven Burns. Most people refer to vampires as 'the undead' but that's not entirely accurate. As Victor tells it, his heart never actually stopped beating. Which is one of the things that made him seem immortal to me. But I suppose everyone and everything dies when it's time. But I digress. Victor had almost nothing when he was changed, but still did not, at first, see the value in his life continuing...especially as it was now. At the very least, he found, he had to have human blood once a month, or he could fall into a coma that he might never awaken from. He did consider the latter option, but some instinct apparently kicked in, and he began to slake his thirst for blood. But he did this by only going after people he perceived to be evil. After all, why should the innocent suffer for his unfortunate circumstances?

After Victor was turned, he had stopped aging. A side-effect of vampirism, I suppose. Over the years, he turned his thirst for human blood into a sort of war on crime. Again, he only preyed on people he considered to be evil. If he found himself thirsty, but only found those he thought of as innocent, he would wait. And he always drank enough blood to kill his victim, instead of turning them into vampires like himself. He had decided that no one else should suffer his particular fate. Of course, his master, Steven, had no such morals. He was still creating vampires in 1949. The two met up, and fought, but Steven was more skilled than Victor. After the bloody battle, Victor found himself missing his left hand. But he was able to regenerate it within weeks. Something to do with healing and shape-shifting, I believe. Now, how do I know all of this? Well, I started writing it down in a journal shortly after Victor and I met in 1989. He told me a number of his past stories. He even told me that Dracula exists, although I have never personally met him. Not that I would really want to, from what I've heard. I remember jokingly referring to Victor once as 'a Nosferatu', but he said that someone made that term up. The technical term, Victor said, is 'homo-vampiri'. I never looked it up, so I took his word for it. But I'm getting ahead of myself. I was just getting around to telling the story of how Victor and I met.

Victor had been hearing stories of vampires in a small town in upstate New York. He had already fought some vampires in his home state in the past, so he did some investigating. Turns out, these were not really vampires at all, but merely humans that play-acted at being vampires. Putting on make-up, wearing fangs, that sort of thing. They did drink blood every now and then, but that is because they were kidnapping people from their area and locking them up in a basement...before killing them in a bogus ceremony that they thought would give them real powers. It was pretty sick, actually. I know, because I was one of the people that they kidnapped. I suppose that is the word for it, but in reality, one of them drugged my drink at a college party I was at. I woke up in chains wondering where the heck I was. One of them (not any older than me) told me what they were up to. They didn't figure I would live long enough to tell the tale. These were bored, rich kids who went a little too far in finding something to occupy their time. They even had a name for their gang; "the crimson bats." I'm sure they never figured that a real vampire would find out about their scheme. But sure enough, the night they were planning on sacrificing me, Victor showed up. I was in the basement, so I missed the action. Still, I could hear the screams above me. They must have really been trying to kill him. They should have tried harder. In minutes, it was over. They were all dead, and Victor was on his way down the stairs.

When I first met Victor, he looked human enough. Though he was a bit pale. Oh, and his fangs were real. He just looked at me at first. I thought he might be one of the vampire-wannabe's, but not one that I had seen before. He assured me he was not. Then he showed me, by coming over to me and breaking one of my chains with one hand! Okay, that scared me. Real vampire. If this guy was hungry, I was dead. His smile surprised me.
 "I'm not going to kill you", he said. "Trust me. I already ate enough at the party." I was in shock, so I just moved away from him. But he was holding the other chain that was holding me.
 "Relax. If I wanted you dead, you'd already be dead. All right?"
 "Ha", I replied. "I guess I would be."
 "You know", he continued, "I may have some use for you. Since I can't go out too much in daylight. And I did just save your life."
 "I would say so. Those guys were crazy. But I didn't think vampires could go out in sunlight at all?" I tried to sound like I had regained my composure. Which I had

not.

"Sounds like you have a lot to learn about real vampires. Let's go to your place."

"Mine? Er...sure. I might have to tidy up a bit."

"Well", he said, "It has to be better looking than the mausoleum I've been sleeping in."

"My place it is, then."

I had been staying in an off-campus apartment, since my parents had some money. I just didn't think I'd be bringing any vampires home. Somehow, the topic of our ages came up. I told Victor I was 20, he told me he was 89.

"You certainly don't look 89!"

"No, I suppose I don't. I haven't really aged since I was bitten. And I still want to kill the old creature that changed me into this...thing."

That's when he told me about Steven Burns. He still kept tabs on him when he could. He sounded bitter whenever he mentioned his name, but that was understandable.

"So, kid, do you know anything about vampires?"

"Just what I've read. Oh, and seen in movies. Is any of that true?"

"Some of it is. You'd be surprised. Some people think that if you're bitten by one, a blood-virus changes you. Unfortunately, that's not the case. If it were, I'd think someone would come up with a cure. The truth is a bit more...depressing."

"I'm sorry to hear that...but how bad could it be?"

"You have no idea", continued Victor. "If a vampire bites you...it changes you, right down to your soul, if he does it right. Your heart never stops beating. Ever. You just...change. And you can't die, no matter how much you might want to."

"Wow", was all I could get out. "But...a wooden stake? Won't that kill a vampire?"

"Yes. Silver hurts, but a wooden stake through the heart...I remember how Burns told it to me. It can disconnect the tether from your heart to your soul...that invisible line, that tether; it's the only thing that keeps a vampire alive after he or she becomes one. Disconnect that, and a vampire will leave this life. For good. But it's really the only way."

"Okay, that's a better explanation than one I've ever heard before. A little supernatural though. So, the people back at that house...they'll all become vampires, too?"

"Nah, but only because I took enough blood from each of them to stop their hearts, causing their death. If I wanted another vampire, I know how to do it. It's a certain amount of blood that you take..."

"I'll take your word for it", I said. "It still all sounds supernatural."

"Well it ain't natural, that's for sure. And I never asked for it, but I learned how to live with it. If you can call this living. I can't even put a stake through myself. Probably because that rotten thing, Burns, is still alive. But I'll get him someday. Maybe with your help. I'm gonna teach you about vampires, and how to fight them. Sound like fun?"

"Sure", I replied.

Over the next few months, I learned a lot from Vic about how to kill a vampire. Turns out I'm something of a natural with a crossbow, who knew. As far as my parents knew, I was just going to college. But I was into some serious extracurricular activities. Eventually I did graduate from college, with a degree in philosophy, of all things. After that, Vic and I started hunting together. I was so nervous the first time I met an actual vampire in combat. I wounded it, but Victor got the kill. Meanwhile,

Vic went on his own hunts a couple of times a month, looking for human blood. I stayed away from that. I figured the less I knew, the better. At first it was twice a month, but as the years passed, he went hunting on his own more frequently. I started losing track of the number of vampires we killed, we were pretty efficient together. In 1999, Victor finally found out where Steven Burns was hiding. By this time, he had heard of us and was trying to maintain a low profile. But we got one of his vampire slaves to talk, which wasn't easy. We had planned to go after him one night when it got especially dark out. No visible moon that night. And Vic had already explained to me that sunlight was like a slow poison to a vampire. It wouldn't kill them, but it would slow them to a crawl. Which is why they avoided it. We went over our plan, and decided it was now or never. Well, Victor decided; he had been growing more restless and ruthless over time. I had noticed, but decided not to mention it to him.

We got into Burns' place pretty easily, he only had one vampire guarding the back door. We dispatched him and headed inside. I figured it for a trap, but the truth was something different. Steven was alone when we found him. He did seem to put up a decent fight at first, but he didn't really seem to be trying. I guessed later that he was growing weary of running from Victor and I, and perhaps he was weary of his own existence. He was easily twice as old as Vic. In any matter, I was able to slow him down. Enough for Victor to finally deliver the killing blow with a wooden stake we had saved for this occasion. Steven howled as he died, but didn't turn into smoke, nothing quite that dramatic. Instead, his body revealed its true age before us, and started to crumble away within minutes. Victor's victory howl was louder than I had ever heard. And he was laughing. I had hoped he finally felt free after all of these years of trying to kill his 'creator'. I was wrong again.

As the months passed, he seemed to get worse than ever. More feral, more ruthless...and now he was hunting for human blood more often than ever before! It was almost like he was becoming Steven. It got to it's lowest point when he finally killed an innocent person so he could feed. This was no criminal, it was a teenage girl. He told me when he came home one morning, and at first he seemed upset. But that night, when I questioned him about it, he replied that it "wasn't a big deal". I could see that he was losing it, and I knew something had to be done.

By the time that the year 2000 rolled around, Vic had become impossible to live with. I feared not only for my own safety, but for others as well. I never should have let him live this long. The only reason I did was that he saved my life all those years ago. But I had known Victor Vanashez for many years now, and I knew this wasn't what he wanted, the way he was living. He had become little more than an animal. Still, being only human, I knew there was no way I'd ever be able to beat him in combat. So one day, while he slept, I chained him to the pipes in the basement. It reminded me all too much of the way that he had found me. I found it distasteful, but didn't feel as if I had much choice. Still, I didn't stake him in his sleep. I waited until he awoke. And as you can guess, he was angry with me.

"Foolish human", he hissed. "What do you think you are doing? I will destroy you for this! Do you think these chains can hold me?"

"Not for long, but they don't really have to. I just wanted to say goodbye to my friend. I'm so sorry this is the way it has to be." By this time, he had already broken one chain. His other wrist was shape-shifting it's way out of it's chain. Sometimes vampires give me the creeps.

Okay, most times.

 "I'm coming for you, human. The only way to stop me is to kill me!"
 "I know", I replied. "I guess I've always known. I am sorry, Victor." I fired my crossbow, and the wooden bolt made its' way to Victor's heart. I can't describe the sound he made, but it wasn't nice. But as he died, he spoke.
 "Thank you, Frank. It's finally over."
 Those words chill me to this day. It was pretty obvious that he left himself wide open for me to kill him. He knew what he had become, and knew that I, and the world, would be better off without him. Still, I miss him. He was the best vampire-hunter there ever was. And he was my best friend. Since then, I've retired from the hunt. They don't even come after me any more, that's how good I was. But eventually, I'll age. And they won't. So, while my tale hasn't yet ended, it almost certainly will soon. I only hope that Victor somehow found peace after all those years of suffering. I miss you, Victor. But I might be seeing you again, some night when the moon is full, and my luck finally runs out.

-THE END.